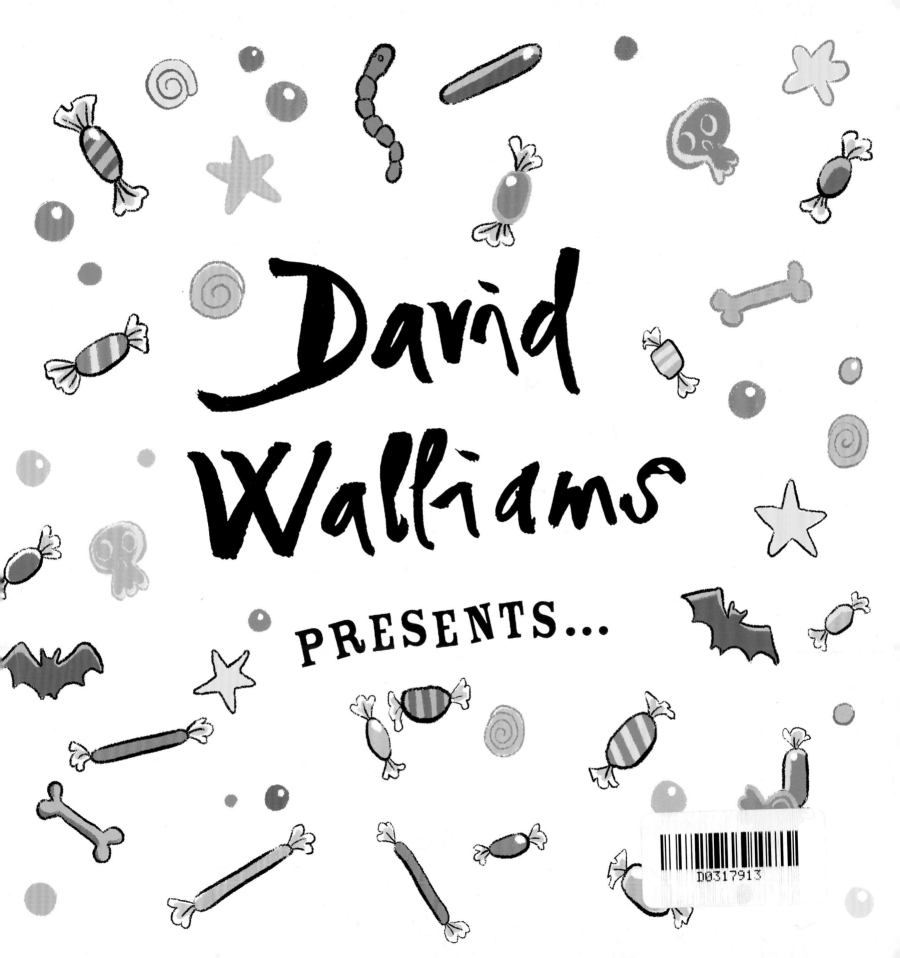

David Walliams

PRESENTS...

For Rockefeller,
with oodles of love,
Uncle David x

For Zoë,
with love – A.S.

First published in hardback in the United Kingdom by
HarperCollins *Children's Books* in 2020
First published in paperback in 2022
This edition published in 2023
HarperCollins *Children's Books* is a division of HarperCollins*Publishers* Ltd
1 London Bridge Street, London SE1 9GF
www.harpercollins.co.uk
HarperCollins*Publishers*
Macken House, 39/40 Mayor Street Upper, Dublin 1, D01 C9W8, Ireland
1 3 5 7 9 10 8 6 4 2
Text copyright © David Walliams 2020
Illustrations copyright © Adam Stower 2020
Cover lettering of author's name copyright © Quentin Blake 2010
ISBN: 978-0-00-858142-8

Printed in Italy

LITTLE MONSTERS

ILLUSTRATED
BY THE AMAZING

*Adam
Stower*

HarperCollins *Children's Books*

Once upon a time, there was a little werewolf with a BIG problem.

His voice was really, really SQUEAKY.

"WOOHO

Whenever there was a **full moon**, **Howler** howled so **high** . . .

"HOOHOOHOo!"

. . . that all the other werewolves howled with laughter.

"HA! HA! HA!"

Howler hated feeling like the **odd one out**. So Papa werewolf and Mama werewolf sent their son off to Monster School where he could learn how to be frightening.

MONSTER SCHOOL

TOWN

Woods

But Howler found the **school** frightening.
He wasn't sure **WHO** to be
more afraid of . . .

the **teachers** . . .

or the **pupils**.

Howler took a seat at the back of the classroom.
Suddenly, his teacher whooshed in on her broomstick,
SMASHING the skeleton to pieces as she did so.

CLA

"The first lesson of the day," announced
Miss Spell, "is how to pull a SCARY FACE.
Show me your scariest one!"

The vampire
flashed his fangs.

The ghost grinned a
ghoulish grin.

T T E R !

The **skeleton** showed a sinister **smile**.

All eyes turned to Howler . . .

"You!" snarled Miss Spell,
pointing at her new pupil.

"Y-y-yes, miss!"

"Show me your
SCARIEST face!
NOW!"

The little werewolf did his best.

He **bulged out** his eyes,

waggled his ears

and **stuck out** his tongue.

Instead of looking **scary**, he looked like he was **blowing off**.
All the other little monsters HOOTED with laughter.

"HA! HA! HA!"

"You couldn't scare a FLY!"
mocked the teacher.

"The second lesson of the day is SPOOKING!" announced Miss Spell in the school hall.

The witch ordered the mummy to **stand still** with his back turned.

One by one,
 the little monsters
 did their best to
 creep up on him.

The vampire
flew.

The ghost
floated.

The skeleton rattled.

Finally, it was Howler's turn.
The little werewolf was so **nervous**
he **tripped** up over his tail.

TRIP!

He t**um**bled over
and over again . . .

ROLL!

. . . landing by the
skeleton's feet.

THUD!

"HA! HA! HA!
You couldn't scare a FLEA!"
snorted Spell.

Next, the teacher led
the little monsters
down steep stone steps.

"The final lesson of the day is
gruesome GROWLS," she said, her voice
echoing around the dark dungeon.

Oh no! thought the little werewolf
with the squeakiest voice.
My worst nightmare!

"HISS!"
went the vampire.

"WUHUHUH!"
went the ghost.

"SNARL!"
went the skeleton.

"HOWLER!"
barked the teacher. "Your turn!"

"B-b-but . . . !"

"NOW!"
demanded the witch.

Trembling with fear, Howler howled **higher** than ever.

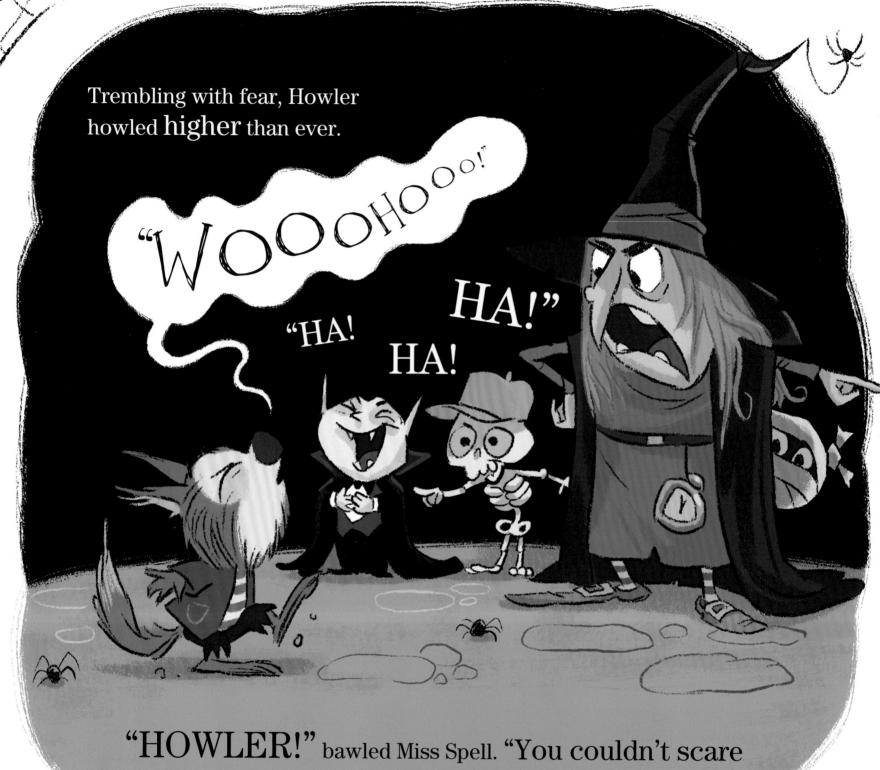

"WOOOHOOo!"

"HA! HA!"

"HA!"

"HOWLER!" bawled Miss Spell. "You couldn't scare
a NIT! You're a disgrace to Monster School!
To the headmaster's office! AT ONCE!"

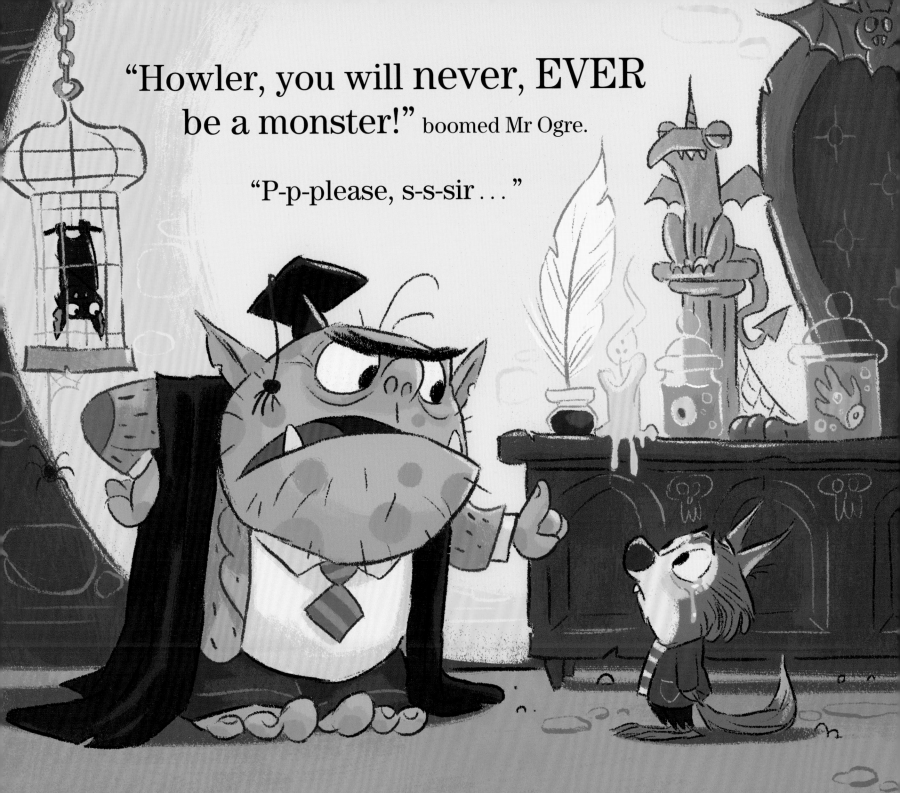

"Howler, you will never, EVER be a monster!" boomed Mr Ogre.

"P-p-please, s-s-sir..."

"YOU ARE EXPELLED FROM MONSTER SCHOOL!"

A **tear** welled in Howler's eye.

Skulking back home to the forest, the werewolf spotted another group of little monsters going door to door and saying,

"TRICK OR TREAT?"

These monsters were **different**. As he drew closer, Howler saw that they were little **humans** dressed up as MONSTERS.

It was HALLOWEEN!

"WOW! Cool werewolf costume!" said an alien on spotting him.

"Are you on your own?" asked a spider.

Howler nodded sheepishly.
None of the kids realised Howler
was a **real-life** werewolf.

"Come and join us!" said a shark.

"Thanks!" exclaimed Howler, smiling for the **first time** in ages.

"You look so SCARY! You can go at the front!" said the alien.

Howler wasn't so sure. He gulped before he knocked on the first door, sure he couldn't even scare a nit.

Knock! Knock! Knock!

But before the werewolf could even say "TRICK OR TREAT?" the man at the door screamed. "ARGH!"

He threw a hail of sweets at the little monsters.

The kids caught them and were over the moon. They had never had so many treats.

With Howler leading the pack, the same thing happened at house after house.

"HELP!"

"NOOO!"

"YIKES!"

Soon **more** and **more** little monsters from **all over town** joined in the FUN.

As **no one** dared to say "TRICK" to the little werewolf, there were **treats** for **everyone!**

Now it was **late** and they'd knocked on all the doors.
The little monsters were stuffed full of sweets
and ready to head home to bed. But there was still
one more person Howler was determined to scare.

Can you **guess WHO?**

"Just ONE more!
Follow me!" he said.

Soon they had reached MONSTER SCHOOL.

"When I hold up my paw,
I want you ALL to do your LOUDEST howl!"
announced Howler.

All the kids grinned from ear to ear.
This was going to be FUN!

"*SHUSH!*" hissed Howler as they crept into the classroom
where Miss Spell was busy marking homework.
Howler raised his paw, and he led them
all in the LOUDEST howl.

"WooHOOHOoHOOHOOHOOHOO!"

"ARGH!"

screamed the teacher,
shooting out of
her chair.

WHOOSH!

She bounced off the ceiling...

BOING!

...she bounced off the walls...

BOING!

BOING!

...she bounced off the floor...

BOING!

. . . before bouncing **right into** the **headmaster**, who had appeared at the door.

WaLLOP!

"WHAT IS THE MEANING OF THIS?"
thundered Mr Ogre as the little monsters helped him up.

"It looks like I CAN scare, after all, sir!" replied Howler.

The headmaster looked down at the crumpled witch by his feet.
Miss Spell was out cold!

"Howler! I was wrong.
You ARE scary!
May I welcome you back to
Monster School?"

The little werewolf looked round at the kids in costumes . . .

"No thanks! I am going to stick with my new friends."

All the little monsters broke out into a howl of happiness.

"WOOHOO!"

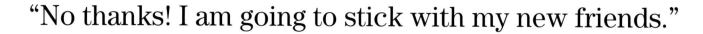

What about **Papa werewolf** and **Mama werewolf**?
They couldn't have been happier that their son
was happy just being himself.

Howler **did** go to school with his **new friends**.

So when YOU are at school have a look around your classroom.

Sitting at the back there **might** just be a little monster.

It's cool to be the ODD one out.

"ARGH!"

"WOOHOOHOOHOOHOOHOO!"